To all the little chickies out there
who are nervous on their first day of school,
but especially to Maki and Santi—twins
who know what it's like to get separated!
—S. J.

For my sister, who always teaches her
chickies to be kind and brave.
—A. G.

Published by Roaring Brook Press
Roaring Brook Press is a division of Holtzbrinck
Publishing Holdings Limited Partnership
120 Broadway, New York, NY 10271 • mackids.com

Our books may be purchased in bulk for promotional, educational, or business use please
contact your local bookseller or the Macmillan Corporate and Premium Sales Department
at (800) 221-7945 ext. 5442 or by email at MacmillanSpecialMarkets@macmillan.com

Library of Congress Cataloging-in-Publication Data is available.

First edition, 2023
Printed in China by RR Donnelley Asia Printing Solutions Ltd.,
Dongguan City, Guangdong Province

ISBN 978-1-250-87202-9
10 9 8 7 6 5 4 3 2 1

This book was designed by Angie Monroy and Monica Matiz,
and edited by Carolina Dammert and Olivia Conley.

Special thanks to Steven Wolfe Pereira, Julie Fleischer, Taylor Margis Noguera,
Connie Hsu, Luisa Beguiristaín, Andrea Mosqueda, Sharismar Rodriguez,
Allene Cassagnol, Jennifer Healey, and Avia Perez.

Go to School

written by **Susie Jaramillo**   illustrated by **Abigail Gross**

Roaring Brook Press
New York

Encantos

It was the first day of school for Kiki and her brothers, Nicky and Ricky.

I feel butterflies in my belly! Kiki thought.

Nicky was ready for the year.

Ricky wanted to be prepared for anything
but needed a bigger backpack!

Once the chickies were ready, the family ran out the door.
Kiki was so happy to go to school with her brothers!

But when they got there, Kiki noticed something funny . . .
Ricky and Nicky were going one way, and she was going another.

"Come on, little one," Mama Hen said.
"You're going to do great on your own!"

Kiki nervously peeked into the classroom.
Her teacher gave her a warm wave of welcome.

With the class gathered for circle time, Kiki's teacher, Pin Pon, introduced himself and his assistant, Lili the spider.

As Kiki looked around, Pin Pon said,
"Class, please tell us what your favorite color is!"

Yaya loved bright pink,
like the roses in her
mom's garden.

Bry said green because he
liked green bugs.

Kit's favorite was orange because it's the color of his basketball!

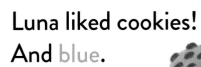

Luna liked cookies!
And blue.

*These chickies are not
so different from me,*
Kiki thought.
I like all those things too!

It was Kiki's turn to answer, but she didn't know how.

Kiki whispered to Pin Pon, "I like all colors!
Would that be okay to say?"

"That sounds like a great answer, Kiki!"
he whispered back.

Kiki smiled and proudly announced,
"My name is Kiki, and I love rainbows!"

Next it was time for arts and crafts.
Lili gave a few pointers.

"I like shiny things," Kiki said.
"I'm going to make a star!"

But when Kiki needed the sparkliest glitter,
she saw that Kit was using it.

Will Kit share if I ask? she thought worriedly.

Kiki finally found the courage to ask,
and Kit kindly gave her the glitter!
But then . . .

With one sneeze, Kiki had covered everything—and everyone—at her table in the sparkliest glitter.

She felt so embarrassed.

"Thanks!" Kit exclaimed. "I wanted
my picture to be more sparkly!"

When Bry and Yaya surprised Kiki by helping her clean up, she was happy.

She made a mess, but she also made three new friends!

When lunchtime came around,
the chickies ran outside to eat.

Kiki opened her lunch box and found a surprise!

Mama's note made Kiki
feel warm and fuzzy.

The rest of Kiki's school day was full of excitement!

She shared her snack with Luna . . .

searched for bugs with Bry . . .

read about the moon with Yaya . . .

and counted flowers with Kit. "Oops, I lost count!"

Before Kiki knew it, the school day was over.
She ran to hug her brothers and Mama Hen.

They asked about her day, and Kiki said proudly,
"I made a big mess, a shiny star, and new friends!"

Kiki felt happy as Mama Hen tucked the chickies into bed that night. She was excited for her next day at school.

It was going to be a wonderful year!